Undercover Christmas Prince

EMORIE COLE

KEWEENAW
PUBLISHING

Jeff

The air is cold, but not too bitter, on my face as snowflakes softly fall all around me while I stroll through the neighborhood in Bessemer. Twinkling Christmas lights drape the houses in festive color, their shimmering reflections dancing across the snow-covered lawns and glistening ice like a thousand tiny stars that have come to life. I pull my jacket and scarf tighter around myself as I continue to walk down the snowy street, thinking about how lucky I am to have found this quaint little town in Upper Michigan—completely by chance—while searching for remote vacation destinations that offer both skiing and holiday festivities.

I smile as I pass a couple of jolly looking snowmen standing tall in one of the yards. They're decorated with fuzzy scarves and hats that match the mittens attached to their oddly long, stick arms. "What a beautiful night, Nigel. Just take a moment and listen—you can hear the church bells playing *Silent Night* softly off in the distance. Isn't this place charming?" I ask my bodyguard who's trailing behind me.

"Yes, Your Highness, quite charming—but don't you think that we ought to be heading back to the chalet? You need to get some rest if you want to go skiing first thing in the morning."

I let out a long sigh. "Very well. But try to remember, Nigel—on this vacation I'm not Prince Jeffrey or 'Your Highness'—I'm just plain old Jeff."

"Right—and I'm not your bodyguard, I'm your good friend that you've known since childhood."

"You've *always* been my best friend, Nigel. We've grown up together since we were babies; even though you protect me, there isn't a single person that I consider a better friend than you."

"Thank you, Sir—I mean—Jeff."

"That's more like it," I say with a grin as I pat him on the back. "Alright, come on, let's head back." We walk back down the street to the chalet that we've rented for the duration of our stay. It's not a glamorous chalet by any means, but it's still charming in its own way, and it's exactly what I was looking for in a place to hideout for awhile. When we arrive, I say goodnight to Nigel and head upstairs to get a good night's sleep.

After brushing my teeth and putting on a pair of pajama pants, I climb into bed before turning off the lamp on the nightstand. I lie awake for quite a while, excited about skiing and exploring this lovely little town tomorrow. A smile spreads across my face as I realize that for the first time in my life, I don't have to worry about responsibilities and protocols or the rigid structure that usually governs my every day existence. I'm not sure exactly how long I spend thinking about everything that I want to do while I'm here, but eventually I drift off into a deep sleep.

Morning comes quickly, and I'm awakened by noises coming from downstairs—unlike the palace, the walls here are not soundproofed. As I sit up and stretch, a strong whiff of bacon hits my nose, and I realize that Nigel must be making breakfast. I quickly roll out of bed and shiver as my bare feet hit the cold wooden floor. Reaching into the dresser near the bed, I grab a pair of warm socks and slip them on just as I hear three swift knocks on the door. "One second, I'm coming," I say loudly as I get up and saunter over to the door.

I open it to find Nigel standing on the other side. "Good morning, Your—Jeff," he says after a moment's hesitation. "Glad to see that you're awake. Breakfast is ready."

"It smells wonderful!"

"I've made bacon, eggs, and toast for you this morning. If there's nothing else you need, I'll let you eat while I go gather our things for skiing."

"Don't worry about it, Nigel. I'm perfectly capable of gathering my own skis."

"As you wish—Jeff. In that case, I'll go get myself ready," he says with a smile as he heads out of the room. I take a seat at the table to eat my breakfast alone, realizing that Nigel has already eaten, as usual. I guess convincing him to forget about his duties for a little while might be more challenging than I expected. I shake my head and sigh at the thought as I take a bite of my food.

Once I'm finished eating and Nigel and I have grabbed our gear, we head out in our rented SUV. The small two-lane highway is snow-covered, but it's well-sanded so it's not slippery, making the short drive an easy one, and ten minutes later, we pull into the parking lot at the ski hill—Indianhead Mountain. We climb out of the car and gather our skis, poles, and boots from the back before heading inside the small chalet to purchase our lift passes. Unlike other ski resorts that I've been to, Indianhead Mountain is very cozy. The word mountain may be in the name, but from the trail maps that I've looked at, and the pictures on the wall, it's more of a small hill with runs that can't possibly take more than a few minutes to ski down. When I walk into the chalet, I see that the small two-story building contains a ticket office and a cafeteria on the top floor, and a sign points to an area for ski rentals on the bottom.

As Nigel and I make our way to the counter, the sound of a woman's cheerful laughter fills my ears. I quickly look around to see where the sound is coming from, only for my eyes to catch on the most beautiful woman that I've ever seen. This petite, dark-haired woman has features that remind me of the greek goddesses that I read about when I was younger. Her bright, sparkling hazel eyes seem to dance as she laughs with a group of women that's making their way towards the exit opposite of me— her long, black wavy hair standing out against the neon pink of her ski jacket.

"Jeff," Nigel says quietly as he nudges me with his elbow, "it's our turn."

I slowly tear my eyes away from the woman,

and move towards the counter. "Yes—yes, of course. Sorry about that. Two lift passes, please." The man behind the counter smiles and nods as he prints the passes and hands them over the counter. "Here you are, Nigel," I say as I hand him one of the passes.

"Thank you. A bit distracted, Jeff?" he asks, the corners of his mouth curving up into a grin as we attach our passes to our jackets and sit down to put on our ski boots.

"Me? Distracted? Of course not—I just thought that I caught a glimpse of some paparazzi that were going to ruin this vacation." I keep my eyes down towards my boots, hoping that he'll completely forget about this. "All set?" I ask as I stand up and hand him his ski poles.

"Absolutely," Nigel says with a knowing gleam in his eyes as he walks over to hold the door open.

As we get outside, I gaze out over the hill. "I don't think that I've ever been to a hill where the chalet is on the top, have you Nigel?"

"No, I can't say that I have—but then again, we've never skied anywhere quite so small before."

"That's true." I adjust my goggles over my eyes and put my wrists through the straps of my poles before shouting to Nigel over my shoulder. "See you at the bottom!" I glide effortlessly through the soft, powdery snow, the cold air rushing past my face as I pick up speed, carving down the slope with precision. My skis carve graceful arcs as I shift from side to side, and I quickly reach the bottom of the hill a few minutes later.

When I come to a stop and turn to look around for Nigel, I only have seconds before I hear a loud shriek as someone hits me hard, and we both fall to the ground in a heap of tangled skis and poles. As I try to remove my skis, I notice who it is that ran into me—the beautiful woman in the neon pink ski jacket. "I'm so sorry!" she gasps. "I'm not sure what happened. One minute I was fine, and the next I was losing control and barreling into you."

"It's okay—I'm fine. Are *you* alright?" I ask as I help to untangle our skis.

She nods her head, her cheeks turning an even deeper shade of pink than they already are. "I think so. Just embarrassed, that's all."

"Don't be embarrassed. Accidents happen."

"I know. I'm so clumsy that they happen to me often," she says as a small laugh escapes from between her lips.

I smile as I help her to her feet. "We all have those days."

"Thanks. I'm Sarah Duncan, by the way."

"Nice to meet you, Sarah. I'm Jeff Hastings." We both reattach our skis before skiing over towards the chairlift where Nigel is anxiously waiting. I give him a subtle nod to reassure him that everything is okay before introducing the two of them to each other. Once introductions are finished, I turn to Sarah and ask, "If you don't mind me asking—where are your friends? I thought that I saw you inside earlier with a larger group."

"Yeah, I was. My friends wanted to ski down one of the more difficult runs, but I need more practice before those. We're going to meet up again later."

"Ah, I see. Well, since you're on your own, you're welcome to join Nigel and I until you need to meet up with them."

"Are you sure? I wouldn't want to impose."

"Don't worry—you wouldn't be imposing. You don't mind if she joins us, do you Nigel?"

"Not at all," he says, a genuine smile lighting up his face.

"Okay, then. Thank you—I'd really like that."

"Ride with me?" I ask as I motion towards the chairlift.

"Okay."

"You go on ahead, Nigel. I'll ride up with Sarah."

Nigel obliges and takes the next available chair. A light pink flush colors Sarah's cheeks again as she catches the next chair beside me. "You didn't have to ditch your friend to ride with me, you know. I would have been fine on my own. At least, I think that I could have managed to get on and off the chair without falling again," she adds with a grin.

"Yes, I believe that you *would* be fine on your own, but I'm sure that you're more interesting than Nigel—I've know him forever."

"I guess we'll find out," she says, her soft laugh creating a small cloud of breath in the chilly air.

Silence envelops us both for a minute until Sarah finally breaks it. "Where are you from, if you don't mind me asking? I haven't heard your accent before."

"I'm from a small country in Europe that nobody has ever heard of. It's called Rohemia."

"You're right, I haven't heard of Rohemia before. So, what brings you all the way to the Upper Peninsula?"

"Honestly, I just needed to take a break from my duties for a while. I wanted to get away from everything and go somewhere that would allow me to truly experience the Christmas holiday for a change, instead of being burdened with obligations throughout the entire holiday season."

"Well, you've come to the right place for experiencing Christmas. Everyone here decorates their homes for the big holiday lighting contest so there are a lot of awesome displays to look at, plus there are horse-drawn sleigh rides with caroling and hot chocolate, too."

"That sounds wonderful! I think I saw something about a parade as well?"

"Yeah, Ironwood—the next town over—has a Jack Frost parade every year. It's a lot of fun to watch as long as you don't mind freezing to death," she says with a grin.

"You mean that it gets colder than it is right now?"

"Much colder. This is warm compared to the coldest we've ever gotten, and since the parade is at night, it's definitely always freezing."

My eyes widen, and I shiver at the thought. "Well, then, I guess that I'll have to be sure to wear warmer clothing." Our chair reaches the top of the hill, and we both easily glide off. Once we've skied out of the way of others exiting the chair lift, we join Nigel and take a moment to figure out what we're doing next. "What do you guys think? Should we check out a few of the other runs or stay here?"

Sarah chews on her bottom lip for a moment. "I think that given how clumsy I am, I should probably stick to this run a little bit longer. I don't want you two to be stuck here, though," she quickly adds.

"It's really not that big of a deal. As long as I can get some skiing in, I don't care if it's the same run or different ones."

"It doesn't make a difference to me, either," Nigel says.

"Really?" Sarah asks hopefully.

I nod my head yes. "Come on—let's ski." Sarah smiles happily, gliding next to me as we head back to the top of the run.

The three of us spend the next few hours skiing together, and while we ride the chairlift, Sarah and I spend time getting to know each other—though I'm careful to leave out a few certain details about myself, particularly about me being a prince. I really like Sarah, and I want her to like me for the person that I am, not because of my title.

"I've really enjoyed spending time with you today, Sarah, and I'd like to see you again. What do you think—could we hang out again sometime?" I ask as we take off our skis and walk towards the lodge after our last run.

She hesitates for a moment before answering. "Sure, why not? I had a great time today, too, and I could probably show you all of the best locations to find the holiday experience that you're looking for. Why don't I give you my number, and you can call me when you have time?" I take my cell phone out of my pocket and hand it to her so that she can enter her phone number. "There you go," she says as she hands it back to me a few seconds later.

"Thanks. I'll call you later." I watch as she disappears inside the main lodge. Once she's out of sight, I turn my attention to Nigel. "What do you think, Nigel?"

"I think that Miss Duncan is lovely, Your—Jeff," he says, catching himself at the last second before finishing the phrase that has been ingrained in him since he was old enough to talk. "But I do hope that you're honest about your background with her. If you're serious about her, she deserves to know who you *really* are sooner rather than later."

I shake my head. "We just met a few hours ago. I'm not sure how I feel about her yet, other than that she's nice and I like her."

"Just be careful."

"I will." I pat him on the shoulder reassuringly. "Thanks for always watching out for me."

"Of course."

We decide to call it a day and head back to our chalet to eat a late lunch. I plan to call Sarah later this evening to see if she'll have dinner with me, but first I need to take some time to consider what Nigel said about being honest with her. Even though we just met this morning, I can't deny that I can see a future for Sarah and I together.

Sarah

After leaving Jeff and heading into the chalet, I quickly find my friends Charlotte, Kara, and Carly, all huddled in front of the fire chatting. "Hey ladies, who's hungry? Because I'm starving!" I say loudly as I approach them with a big smile on my face.

"All of us!" they say in unison as if they planned it on cue.

"Well, that settles it then, let's head to 906 Cafe for lunch." We all laugh as we grab our things and head out the door. Once we get to the cafe, the hostess seats us, and our food arrives quickly after we order it. As we start to dig in, I still can't wipe the smile off of my face.

"What's up, Sarah?" Charlotte asks. "You've

had a smile on your face ever since we met back up with you at the lodge after the rest of us finished our double black diamond runs and you got back from wherever it was that you were hiding."

"I wasn't hiding," I grumble. "You know that I'm just too clumsy for the harder runs."

"I know, I was just teasing. Now, quit avoiding the question—why have you had that smile plastered on your face?"

Thoughts of Jeff Hastings, the hunky skier that I spent most of the morning with, keep running through my head. "Have I?" I say naively as if I have no clue what she's talking about.

"Yes, you have," responds Kara.

I take a second while I bite into a French fry to debate whether or not I should tell the girls about Jeff before realizing that there's no point in hiding it. They'll all find out eventually anyways since we live in a small town, especially if I plan on going out with him in public. "Well—I met someone this morning."

"What do you mean you met someone?" asks Carly quizzically.

"I mean—I spent all morning skiing with and talking to this amazing guy named Jeff." I laugh at the memory of our first meeting. "I met him when I literally ran into him at the bottom of the hill."

Charlotte nearly spits out her sip of milkshake as her eyes widen comically. "What?!"

"I sort of lost control on one of my first runs, and I couldn't stop in time. We were a tangled mess of skis and poles. After that, he rode the chairlift with me and invited me to ski with him and his friend since I was alone."

"That was nice of him."

"Yeah, too bad you'll probably never see him again—unless he's a local. But most of the skiers that we don't already know are tourists," Kara says sadly.

"Well—actually I will see him again. We exchanged phone numbers since he wants to hang out with me again—and I kind of offered to show him around town."

"You gave him your number?" asks Carly anxiously. "Do you really think that was a good idea?"

"Relax, Carly," Charlotte says with a smirk. "Not everyone is a psycho stalker. You watch too many crime shows."

"I know," she says a little sheepishly. "But seriously, Sarah. How much do you really know about this guy?"

"I know enough to feel comfortable giving him my phone number. Besides, as much as I like him, I doubt anything serious will happen. He's visiting from Europe, and he has to go home after the holidays."

"He's from Europe?" Kara asks excitedly.

A grin spreads across my face at her enthusiasm. "Mmm-hmm."

"That's exciting!"

"It is, but I don't think that this will turn out to be anything more than a holiday fling, unfortunately. I'm not into long-distance relationships."

I spend the rest of lunch gushing about how dreamy his European accent is and how gorgeous he looks with his green eyes and dark blond hair. By the time that we head home, all of the girls—including Carly—are happy for me, even if Jeff and I end up being just friends. It's been a long time since I've put myself out there with a guy. I may as well enjoy the time that we have together since he's the first guy in a long time to make me feel this happy.

When the girls drop me off at home a little while later, I take a quick shower before changing into my favorite pair of leggings and a comfy sweater. I'm in the middle of trying to tame my wavy, wet hair when my cell phone rings. Picking it up, I see Jeff's name flashing on the screen and let out a happy little squeal before composing myself enough to answer. "Hello?"

"Hi, Sarah. It's Jeff. How are you?"

"I'm great, thanks. What's up?"

"Well, I know that it's short notice, but I was wondering if you would like to join me for dinner tonight? Around seven, perhaps?"

I pause for a moment so as not to seem too anxious, but of course I'm going to say yes. "Sure, I'd love to. Maybe afterwards I can show you where some of my favorite Christmas light displays are."

"That sounds wonderful. Should I pick you up?"

"Sure." I give Jeff my address, and we end our call. I finish drying and styling my hair before rushing to my closet to find the perfect outfit to wear tonight. Something not too flashy, but not too modest either. A soft red sweater dress catches my eye in the closet, with black leggings underneath and a pair of dressier winter boots—the kind that look nice, but will still keep my feet warm and dry.

Once I've decided on my clothes, I spend the

rest of the afternoon relaxing and reading, trying to keep my mind off of my upcoming date. It's been so long since I've been on one, that I'm not quite sure what to expect. When six o'clock rolls around, I change out of my comfy clothes and into the cute outfit that I chose earlier for the night. Glancing into the mirror, I check to make sure that my hair is still cooperating before putting on my makeup—a light pink eyeshadow with just a hint of glitter, some mascara, and my favorite clear lipgloss. I don't bother putting on any blush since I have a feeling that my cheeks will be pink all on their own.

A few minutes before seven, the doorbell rings, and I rush to the door to answer it. When I open it, Jeff is standing on the other side holding a bouquet of red roses. "Hello. I'm sorry if I'm a bit early," he says as he hands me the flowers. "These are for you."

"Thank you. They're beautiful," I say with a smile. "Come inside for a second while I put these into some water and grab my coat."

He steps inside, looking around as I close the door behind him. "You have a lovely home, Sarah."

"Thanks. I moved in a few years ago when I got tired of living in an apartment." I make my way into the kitchen to grab a vase and fill it with water.

Once I've got the flowers arranged on the counter, I walk over to the hall closet to grab my coat.

"Please, allow me to help you with that." Jeff takes my coat and holds it for me to slip into.

I giggle with amusement. "Wow, are all guys from Rohemia such gentlemen?"

Jeff shakes his head. "Not all. I was just raised very proper."

"Well, *I* think that it's charming."

We make our way outside to the waiting car, and Jeff opens the passenger door for me. When he climbs into the driver's seat, he grins. "It's a bit chilly, so I took the liberty of turning on your heated seat and left the car running when I came in to get you."

I smile as I relax into the dark leather seat. "No complaints from me—it feels cozy in here."

"Perfect. Do you have any suggestions for dinner? I did a little research on places to eat around here, but since you're a local, I thought that you might know the best spots."

"Hmm—I guess that it depends on what type of food you're in the mood for. Elk and Hound or Iron Nugget pretty much both have a bit of everything, Jagger's Ore House has great pizza, and if you're in the mood for Mexican food, there's a great little place in Hurley."

"Where's Hurley?" he asks.

"About fifteen minutes from here."

"In that case, I'd love to try Mexican food."

"You've never had Mexican food before?" I ask in disbelief.

"I'm afraid not. I've eaten a large variety of different cuisines in my life, but Mexican has not been one of them."

"I'll fix that," I say with a small laugh as I type the restaurant's name, El Tarasco, into the car's GPS. "I could just tell you how to get there, but this might be easier for you. I tend to give directions more by landmarks rather than by actual street names or cardinal directions."

Jeff chuckles. "Do you really?"

"Yep. It's just a habit of being from a small town, I guess. All of my friends do it, too."

We talk about all of the different types of food that we've both tried as Jeff drives us to the restaurant. Once we arrive, I look at the menu before recommending a few of my favorite items for him to try. "We could try the Molcajete Stone Bowl Special together. I've had it a few times before with my friends, and it's fantastic. It has Ribeye, al pastor meat, grilled chorizo, and even cactus."

"Cactus?! Isn't that a little—prickly?" Jeff asks with a raised eyebrow.

"It has great flavor, you'll love it. I promise."

"If you say so, I'm up to try anything."

The waiter comes to take our order, and once we've made our selections, Jeff and I resume our conversation. "So, do you travel a lot, Sarah?"

I let out a short laugh. "I wish! I have a whole list of places that I'd like to visit someday, but most of them I'll probably only ever dream of. What about you?"

"I've traveled quite a bit actually. Some for pleasure, some for business."

"What type of business?"

He hesitates for a moment, glancing down at his hands before returning his gaze to me. "Let's just say that I'm following in my father's footsteps in the family business. One day I'll take over for him, and I need to be prepared. A lot of the business travel that I do is to attend—how shall I put this—meetings and to learn how he handles certain situations."

"I see. That's great that you want to follow in

his footsteps, though, right? I mean, it's not some shady business is it?"

A laugh bursts out of Jeff, and it takes him a minute to compose himself. The corners of his eyes crinkle as he shakes his head and smiles. "No, it's not shady, I promise. But—"

"But," I prompt.

"But sometimes I wish that I didn't have to take on *all* of the responsibilities that he has. There are incredibly high expectations, and sometimes it's a lot to handle. Like I said this morning, that's part of the reason that I came on this vacation—to get away from it all for a while."

"Well, even so, I'm sure that you'll be great when you take over. You seem like an intelligent, reliable man who's capable of handling responsibilities."

Jeff chuckles again. "You got all of that from knowing me for less than a day?"

I grin. "I've been told that I'm an excellent judge of character, thank you very much."

"Well, not to sound arrogant, but I'd like to think that you're right."

We pause our conversation when our food arrives so that we can dig into the delicious Molcajete. I watch Jeff's face as he takes his first bite of cactus. He closes his eyes as he chews. "This is *so* good," he says as he scoops up another bite along with some ribeye.

I smile. "Good. I'm glad that you like it."

"I think Mexican is my new favorite cuisine. But it sure is spicier than I expected," he says with a sniff.

"Uh-oh. I might have created a monster," I tease. "Since this is the first time that you've eaten it, I'm guessing there aren't any Mexican restaurants where you live. What will you do?"

"I guess that I'll just have to have my chef find some recipes."

My eyes widen. "You have a chef?"

"Oh—um—yeah. Comes with the family business," he says with a shrug.

"That must be nice. I wish I had a personal chef. There are plenty of nights that I just don't feel like cooking, so I end up eating junk food."

Jeff laughs. "Junk food is okay sometimes, though, right?"

I smirk. "Occasionally."

We finish our meal and head outside to the car. "Where to next?" he asks.

"I want to show you my favorite thing to do

around Christmastime—driving around and looking at all of the houses' Christmas lights."

"Sounds good to me. Just tell me where to go."

I direct him to all of the neighborhoods that have the best light displays. We drive all throughout Ironwood, Bessemer, and Wakefield. When we finally pull up in front of my house, it's pretty late. Jeff puts the car into park, and we both just sit quietly for a minute, neither of us moving. "Thanks for such a wonderful night," I finally say.

"I should be the one thanking you. You introduced me to my new favorite food, and provided me with an incredible holiday experience."

"You're welcome."

We both reluctantly climb out of the car, and Jeff walks me to my door. "I really enjoyed tonight, Sarah. Can I see you again tomorrow?" he asks hopefully.

"I have to work during the day, but I'd be up for going on a sleigh ride and caroling if you're interested."

"That sounds fantastic. Text me the details."

"Okay, I will."

I reach into my purse for my keys, but Jeff's gentle touch on my arm stops me. I raise my eyes to his, butterflies in my stomach going crazy as he gazes back at me. "Goodnight, Sarah." He leans down, his lips softly brushing against mine as he kisses me.

"Goodnight," I whisper, a little breathlessly, when we part.

"I'll see you tomorrow," Jeff says with what sounds like a soft chuckle.

"See you then." I unlock my front door and step inside, closing the door behind me. As soon as the lock re-engages, I lean against the door with a silly grin on my face. If someone had asked me this morning what I'd be doing tonight, I never would have guessed that the answer would be falling head over heels for the handsome man that I met on the ski hill, after only one day of getting to know him, and just one sweet kiss later. It sounds absolutely crazy, but that's exactly what I'm doing tonight.

Jeff

As I walk through the door of my chalet, I can still taste the sweetness of Sarah's lips on mine. I hadn't planned on kissing her tonight, especially since we've only known each other for less than twenty-four hours, but I couldn't help it. Desire is still coursing through my body as I think about what else I'd like to do with her, and I know that sleep isn't an option until I do something to—unwind.

I quickly let Nigel know that I've returned before heading into my bathroom to turn on the shower. As I stand under the spray of water a few minutes later, I finally give in to my desires for Sarah and grip my already hard, throbbing cock in my soapy hand. After the thoughts that I've had tonight, paired with the taste of her lips, I'm already at a point where I'm so turned on that I won't be able to last very long. My touch alone has awakened every last nerve ending in my body, making my legs shake and my breath come out in quick, ragged gasps.

Thoughts of caressing Sarah's body run through my mind as I stroke myself, squeezing and tugging as my fist slides up and down my shaft. With each pump of my hand driving me closer towards the edge, I allow myself to imagine what it would be like to suck her hard nipples into my mouth and tease her with my tongue before spreading her legs and sinking myself deep inside of her. My hand quickly pumps the head of my cock a few times before slowly sliding down the shaft, repeating the torturous motion over and over again as I imagine her scratching her nails along the muscles of my back while she trembles from the sensations. The images in my mind are so vivid that it's overwhelming, and I let my eyes close and my head fall back as pleasure courses through me. With a few more pumps, my balls tighten, my muscles shake, and I call out her name with my release as my seed coats my hand. Breathing heavily, I lean my head against the wall, trying to calm myself as I let the water run down my body to rinse myself clean.

I stand in the shower long enough to let my breathing return to normal before stepping out and toweling off. Once I've wrapped the towel around my waist, I return to my bedroom to throw on a pair of boxers and crawl into bed, exhausted from one of the best orgasms that I've ever given to myself. For now, I can only imagine that the real thing with Sarah will be even better.

When I wake up in the morning, I take a few extra minutes to shave the short stubble off of my face in preparation for my date with Sarah tonight. Once I'm finished shaving and getting dressed, I make my way into the kitchen to find Nigel. "Good morning, Nigel!" I say cheerfully.

"Good morning. You're awfully—happy this morning, Your Highness. I take it you had a good night?"

"It was a great night."

"And I'm guessing that you have plans to see Miss Duncan again?" he asks knowingly.

"Yes, as a matter of fact, I do. We're going to attend the Christmas sleigh rides and go caroling."

Nigel smiles. "Well, I'm not thrilled about you gallivanting all over without me, but I *am* glad that you're having a good time—and that you're in good company."

I narrow my eyes at him suspiciously. "You ran a background check on her, didn't you?"

"Of course I did!" he says defensively. "I can't have the Prince of Rohemia running all over a strange town with some unknown woman. The King and Queen would have my head if anything happened to you."

I consider this for a moment before answering. "Very well, I forgive you. But, please, keep the details to yourself—I don't want to know. I want to learn everything about Sarah the old-fashioned way."

"As you wish—Your Highness." I shake my head at his continued use of my official title. At least we're in private so there isn't anyone else around to overhear.

Nigel and I both eat breakfast—I've finally convinced him to eat *with* me instead of *before* me—before heading back to the ski hill for a few hours. With just the two of us today, we spend our time exploring the rest of the slopes that we didn't get to yesterday. When I've eventually had enough skiing for the day, we head back to the chalet so that I can shower and change for tonight. After I'm cleaned up, I double check the text message that Sarah sent earlier to confirm that I have the details correct. I'm to meet up with her at her place at five-thirty so that we can walk to Main Street to go on the sleigh ride.

I pull up in front of her house at exactly five-thirty and knock on the door. When she answers, she's dressed in a pair of jeans, a long winter coat, and a fuzzy hat with matching mittens. "Hey!" she says. "I hope you dressed warm."

"Don't worry—I made sure to put on extra layers," I assure her.

"Perfect. Let's go—we don't want to be late."

She locks her door, and we begin walking down the street. "So, how far is it exactly to where we're going?" I ask.

"Not far. Only a couple of blocks."

"Okay." We walk in silence for a few minutes— the quietness only broken by the crunching snow beneath our boots—as we take in the snowy scene around us. Snowflakes are drifting lazily from the sky, glittering in the warm glow of the streetlights like tiny stars. Each lamppost is wrapped in twinkling lights and adorned with a lush green wreath tied with a velvety red bow that's swaying slightly in the cold breeze. The air smells faintly of pine and woodsmoke, and the windows of houses are sparkling with holiday magic—colorful tree lights and frosted glass. Finally, after much debate about whether or not I should bring it up, I'm the first one to speak. "About that kiss last night—I'm sorry if I was out of line," I say.

Her eyes find mine as a slow smile lights up her face—it's almost as if she's glowing. "You weren't. I wasn't expecting it on our first date, but I liked it."

"I liked it, too." A smile tugs at my lips as I consider the words that I just said. I'm not quite sure that 'like' is even the right word to describe how that kiss made me feel, and I want to discuss it with her more, but before I can continue the conversation, we arrive at Main Street. I guess it's going to have to wait until later.

"Here we are," Sarah says as she leads me towards a crowd of people gathered around a large horse-drawn sleigh filled with blankets.

Sarah introduces me to several people that she knows, and we're both given a small booklet of Christmas carols. We climb up onto the sleigh with the rest of the carolers, the wood creaking softly beneath our boots as we step inside. As the sounds of laughter and cheerful chatter fill the air, we find a cozy spot to sit near the back, nestled between two lanterns that are hung on the arch above the sleigh. Once we're both settled, I reach for one of the thick wool blankets that are folded nearby and shake it out before draping it over our laps. "Thanks," she says quietly.

"Of course." Our knees brush under the warmth of the blanket, and she leans slightly into my side—her proximity is close enough to make my heart race, but seems casual enough to pretend that it's nothing at all.

When everyone has found a seat and the last of the blankets is tucked snugly around another cold caroler, the driver gives a gentle tap of the reins. The horses lift their heads, exhaling little clouds into the frosty night air, and begin to move with a steady, rhythmic clop of their hoofs. The sleigh glides forward with a soft crunch of snow beneath it's runners, and a collective hush falls over the group for just a moment—as if we're all holding our breath and waiting for the magic to begin.

Then, someone starts singing the first notes of *Jingle Bells*, and the rest of us eagerly join in, flipping open the caroling booklets on our laps. Our voices rise together as we wind through the quiet, snow-blanketed neighborhoods. Familiar favorites like *Silent Night* and *Deck the Halls* echo softly through the crisp air—some songs sung more than once, simply because we all love them.

The snow that's falling from the sky lands on us, dusting our coats and hats like powdered sugar and decorating our eyelashes before melting on our cheeks. Families step outside of their homes to listen —mothers with steaming mugs in hand and children bundled up in scarves and mittens, waving with sleepy smiles on their faces. Some of them join in, their joy contagious as they sing or hum along to the tunes.

With every step that the horses take, the bells on their harnesses chime a soft, melodic jingle that weaves through our songs, adding the perfect rhythm to the night. It feels like something that I've read about in storybooks—nostalgic, enchanting, and just a little bit unreal. It makes me feel like anything is possible right now—maybe even that what Sarah and I share is something real...something like true love.

I wrap my arm more tightly around her and smile, completely captivated by the sound of her beautiful voice as she sings. When our eyes meet, there's something in her gaze—something soft and open—that makes me wonder if she feels the same way that I do. And in that moment, the warmth that rushes through me is better than any blanket could ever be.

Pushing my thoughts aside, tucking them away for later, I turn my attention back to the present— joining in again with all of the cheerful caroling and soaking in all of the holiday charm around us. Once we've visited all of the neighborhoods along the planned route, the sleigh circles back to Main Street where we are able to disembark and enjoy hot chocolate provided by the volunteers. When it's our turn, I climb down first, then reach up to take Sarah's hand in mine, steadying her as she steps down beside me. Her fingers linger just long enough to make my heart stutter, and it takes me a second to steady myself again.

When I'm finally able to remember how to breathe properly, I make my way over to the volunteer stand to collect our hot chocolate. "Thank you," I say to them as I take two steaming cups from the table and hand one to Sarah.

She smiles and takes it gratefully. "Thanks. I love hot chocolate on a cold night."

"Me, too."

We sip the hot liquid slowly, letting it's warmth seep through our fingers and chase away the lingering chill in our bones. A few of the other carolers have stuck around, too, and we visit with them for a while—sharing stories, swapping compliments on singing voices, and smiling at the way the night seemed to wrap us all in it's magical, festive glow. After finishing the last sips of our drinks and exchanging cheerful goodbyes, we finally turn to go, starting the walk back to Sarah's house. She falls into step beside me, our hands lightly brushing occasionally, and I glance over with a smile. "Thank you for inviting me to join you. That was a lot of fun."

"You're welcome, Jeff. I had a great time, too."

"Do you do that every year?"

"I try to, if I'm around. My friends and I have gone out of town for the holidays a couple of times."

"Well, I'm glad that you didn't go out of town *this* year."

"Me, too. If I had, I would never have met you." My heart beats a little faster at her words, hope springing up inside of me. When we reach her house, I walk her to the door, and she pauses for a moment, as if debating something with herself. "Would you like to come inside?"

I really shouldn't—every emotion in me is pulling too strongly, and I'm not sure if I can keep my hands to myself at the moment—but before I can stop myself, the word slips out. "Sure."

We step inside, stomping the snow off of our boots and removing our outdoor gear in the entryway before walking into her cozy living room. "Make yourself at home," she says, motioning to the couch. "Can I get you something to drink?"

"No, thanks. I'm fine."

"Okay," she says as she joins me on the couch, fidgeting nervously.

I gently put my hand on her shoulder to still her. "Are you okay, Sarah?"

"Yeah, sorry. I'm just a little bit nervous, I guess. It's been a while since—since I've invited a guy inside after a date. Actually—until our date last night, it's been a while since I've had one of those, too."

"There's no reason to be nervous. We can move at whatever speed that you feel comfortable with. I'm never going to pressure you into anything, and besides—we haven't even established what this thing between us is yet."

She smiles. "That's part of why I'm so nervous. I know that we just met, and maybe we should take things slow—that is, if you're even *interested* in being anything more than friends with me—but the truth is, I don't *want* to take things slow. Being with you feels easy, natural. Like something that I wasn't expecting but somehow always needed. And I know that it's fast, but this just feels right to me."

My eyes flick back and forth, searching her face, and I can tell that she's being sincere. I'm not going to lie—knowing that she wants this as much as I do turns me on, and so for the first time in my life, I decide that I'm going to be spontaneous and worry about the possible consequences later. Before I can overthink it, I lean in and crush my lips against hers. This time she's ready for it, and she parts her lips to allow my tongue to slide in and tangle with hers. I wrap my fingers into her wavy hair, gently tugging, positioning her head to allow me to deepen the kiss. She moans softly into my mouth, while her hands slide up my chest, gripping my shirt, pulling me closer.

Breaking my lips away from hers, I trail kisses down her neck to her shoulder, and she shivers. "Tell me if you want me to stop," I mumble as I slide the fabric of her shirt out of the way to continue worshiping her, my mouth sliding lower with each nip of my teeth and gentle caress of my lips.

"Don't stop," Sarah says breathlessly. "I don't want you to stop."

"Are you sure?" My hand dips into her lacy bra, cupping her breast in my hand as I free it from the fabric and slide to my knees in front of her. My gaze meets hers as my tongue darts out, licking her now exposed nipple before sucking it into my mouth.

Her head falls back, eyes closed, as she lets out a whimper. "Yes—yes, I'm sure," she gasps.

I trail my hand down as I keep my mouth occupied with her other nipple, lavishing it with the same attention as the first. When I reach the button of her jeans, I pop them open, allowing my my fingers to dip just beneath the waistline of her panties before slowly running them lower. She hisses out a breath, her hips lifting off of the couch, as my fingers brush against her sensitive clit. My cock is hard, pressing uncomfortably against the confines of my jeans, and I can feel the pre-cum leaking from the tip as I listen to all of Sarah's delicious moans. After swirling my fingers around her bundle of nerves several more times, I slide them down to push gently against her entrance, allowing one to slip inside. I groan as I tear my lips away from her breast. "Oh, fuuuck—you're so wet."

Her breathing becomes quicker as I add a second finger, pumping them both in and out, in and out, keeping a slow, steady rhythm. "I want you, Jeff," she says, her voice shaky and full of desire.

"Not until after I've tasted you." Taking a moment to tug her jeans and panties off, I toss them to the floor before replacing my fingers with my tongue. My name explodes from her lips as she moans at the contact. I lick and suck, teasing her, driving her higher as my mouth explores. When I finally suck her clit into my mouth, it pushes her over the edge and she trembles as she slowly comes down from her orgasm.

"Where's your bedroom?" I ask, swiping the back of my hand across my mouth.

She smiles at me, cheeks flushed and eyes still full of lust. "Down the hall on the left."

I scoop her up into my arms and carry her into the bedroom, gently placing her on the bed when we get there. She reaches for my pants, quickly unbuttoning them, and sliding them down my legs, followed by my boxers, causing me to chuckle at her impatience. Her eyes linger just below my waist as my cock springs free. "Like what you see?" I ask

"Mmm-hmm. Now, come here."

I do as she says and slowly climb on top of her. I know that she's extremely wet and ready for me after the orgasm that she just had, so I waste no time. Wrapping my hand around my erection, I line it up, the broad head of my cock nudging against her entrance, and push in with one quick thrust, filling her up completely. We both let out a loud moan of pleasure at the new sensation. "You're so tight, so wet." I close my eyes, cursing and hoping that I can last more than a few seconds with her walls gripping me so tightly.

Once she's had a moment to adjust to my intrusion, I begin to rock my hips against hers in a slow, steady rhythm. When she hooks her legs around my waist, pulling me deeper inside, I let out a long groan as she tightens even more around me. "You like that?" she asks.

"You have no idea how impossibly good that feels." I release a shaky breath before closing the small distance between us, pressing my lips to hers —pouring every ounce of the passion that she makes me feel into the kiss.

We're both breathing heavily as I thrust into her

again and again, swirling my hips and trying to keep my rhythm steady, until she's trembling beneath me. Her nails rake over my back when I slip my hand between our bodies and begin circling her clit—the feeling in reality even better than what I imagined in the shower—sending shivers up my spine. We shift position, the new angle allowing me to slide in even deeper, changing the sensations for both of us yet again. "Jeff!" she gasps. When she cries out my name with her second release of the night, I lose all of the control that I've been barely managing to hold onto. My thrusts become quicker and more erratic as I pound into her—harder, faster —until I'm calling out her name with my own release.

My forehead rests against hers, my weight supported on my elbows, as we remain tangled together for a few moments, trying to regain our composure. When we're finally able to pull our sweaty bodies apart, I roll off of Sarah and collapse onto the bed next to her. "Wow," she says happily beside me. "That was—incredible."

I roll onto my side to face her and push a strand of hair off of her face, tucking it behind her ear. "I think that *you're* incredible, Sarah."

"I think that you are, too," she whispers softly.

I hold her gaze for a moment before deciding that I need to come clean and tell her who I really am. I really should have told her before things ever got this far, but I selfishly didn't want to risk losing her—although this has the potential to make me lose her anyway. Taking a deep breath, I take her hand in mine and hold it between us. "Sarah, there's something that I need to tell you. I probably should have told you sooner, and for that, I'm sorry."

A look of panic crosses her face—her wide eyes begin to glisten and her jaw tightens. It's like she's trying to hold herself together while something inside of her unravels. "Oh, no. Please, please don't tell me that you're married or something. That would be just my luck—the first time that I decide to do something crazy and sleep with someone that I've practically just met, and he turns out to be married. I can't be the other woman, I just can't."

I squeeze her hand gently to reassure her. "Calm down—no, I'm not married. It's nothing like that. It's nothing bad either."

Her expression softens again, replaced by a slight look of confusion instead. "Okay, what is it then?"

"I haven't been completely honest about who I really am."

"You're not Jeff Hastings?"

"I am—but my full name is Jeffrey Edward Samuel Hastings—the third—Prince of Rohemia."

She stares at me for a minute, a look of amusement on her face. "Ha ha, very funny. Who are you, really?" I continue to gaze into her eyes, not saying anything as she processes the truth. "You're joking, right?"

I shake my head. "No, I'm afraid not. You can look me up on the internet if you wish. Or ask Nigel—he's my best friend—but he's also my bodyguard. I'm sorry that I didn't tell you when we first met."

"Why didn't you?"

"Because usually when people know that I'm a prince they treat me differently. I just wanted you to like me for me, not because I'm royalty."

"I *do* like you for you, Jeff."

"Really?" I ask, disbelief and hope warring within me.

She nods her head yes. "Nothing will ever change that. I never would have treated you differently, either. That's not who *I* am. Title or no title, you're still just a person."

"I know that now," I say sheepishly. "I truly am sorry for not trusting you with my identity sooner."

"It's okay. Just promise me that from now on you'll be honest with me. No more secrets."

I give her a quick kiss. "Deal."

Sarah cuddles against me, and I breathe a sigh of relief that she's not mad at me—and that my title didn't scare her off. Now that she knows the truth, I can finally discuss the future with her like I've been wanting to.

Sarah

It's warm and cozy waking up in Jeff's arms, and as I slowly open my eyes, I see him sleeping peacefully next to me. I can't help but smile when I think about last night. The way that he makes me feel is indescribable—like nothing I've ever felt before—and I don't want to lose this feeling. I admit that his confession about being a prince was shocking to say the least, but I'm not going to hold the fact that he kept his identity a secret from me against him. I understand why he did it, and I can't say that I wouldn't do the same if our roles were reversed. Snuggling in closer to him, I rest my head against his shoulder, and sigh happily. No matter what, to me, he's still just Jeff. The man that I've fallen head over heels for.

He begins to stir beside me, which gives me an idea. Deciding to go for it, I lean over to kiss him. When my hands begin trailing down his bare chest, slowly moving lower and lower, he moans against my lips, and as I lightly brush against his cock—already somewhat hard—he lets out a curse before opening his eyes.

"This is a nice way to wake up," he says sleepily, lust already clouding his eyes.

"Mmm—you like that?" I ask as I wrap my hand around him and begin gently stroking.

"Very much." His breathing quickens with each stroke of my hand, soft moans falling from his lips as I twist gently with each up and down movement. My thumb collects the fluid from his leaking tip, spreading it around the head in slow, circular patterns. His eyes stay locked on mine as I begin trailing kisses down his bare chest. My mouth continues to move lower, exploring his stomach, inching towards his hips. "Don't stop," he begs as my hand stills.

"Don't worry—I won't," I say as my tongue darts out to lick the tip of his cock.

He hisses out a breath. "Oh, fuck!" I smile against him as I wrap my mouth around his thick length. His fingers tangle in my hair as I lick and suck, teasing him with my tongue, sliding it up from balls to tip, fluttering against the sensitive bottom part of the head before repeating the trail in reverse. I can feel his muscles trembling as I hollow my cheeks, creating more suction as I pull him into my mouth, alternating between sucking fast, and then slow, then fast again. As I drive him closer to the edge, he gently stops me before pulling me on top of him. "As much as I love having your pretty lips wrapped around my cock, this will be over too soon for both of our liking if you keep doing that. I want you, Sarah. Please?"

I nod my head yes—I'm already dripping wet from pleasuring him—and he wastes no time lining himself up with my entrance and pulling me down onto his cock. We both let out a moan as waves of pleasure flood through us. As I rock back and forth, he places his hands on my hips to help guide them —but still lets me dictate the pace—before sucking my nipple into his mouth. I ride him, his cock filling me slowly and deeply each time that I slide down, my clit rubbing against his body as I swirl my hips at the end of every downstroke. The sound of flesh hitting flesh fills the room as our hips rock together, faster, harder. My movements become more erratic as I get closer, and he wraps his arms around me, flipping us so that I'm on my back and he's on top. Taking over, he thrusts into me, again, and again, and again. We're both breathing hard as he slams into me one last time, sending us both over the edge.

As we lie next to each other afterwards, Jeff says, "You're amazing—you know that?" He beams at me as if I'm the only one in the world.

A matching smile lights up my face. "So are you."

He takes my hand in his, taking a deep breath before meeting my eyes. "I think that I'm falling in love with you, Sarah."

I search his face, seeing nothing but sincerity in his eyes. "I think that I'm falling in love with you, too, Jeff."

"Then come back to Rohemia with me."

"What?" I stutter as shock spreads through me. I must have heard him wrong—there's no possible way that he just asked me what I *think* he just asked me. Is there?

He smiles. "I want to spend more time getting to know you, Sarah. I want to show you where I grew up, show you all of the beauty that Rohemia has to offer."

"I don't know," I say hesitantly. "What about my family, my friends, my job?"

"I know that I'm asking a lot of you, but just think about it, okay? You told me that you've dreamt about traveling—this could be your chance. I could take you to places that you've never been to. Your family and friends are always welcome to visit, and you can always come back here whenever you want."

I nod. "I'll think about it."

He gives me another passionate kiss, and pulls me closer—both of us enjoying the feel of being in each other's arms after admitting our feelings for one another. When we finally pull apart, he says, "As much as I don't want to go, Nigel is probably wondering where I am. I'm actually kind of surprised that he didn't bang down your door last night looking for me."

I sigh. "I don't want you to leave either, but my family is probably waiting for me, too. We have plans today."

"Alright. I'll see you later for the parade?"

"Of course."

We crawl out of bed and get dressed before leaving my house and going our separate ways. As I head over to my parents' house, I think about how I'll break the news to them about Jeff. He agreed with me that I need to tell them who he is —the full truth—and that I should talk to them about everything before I make my decision about going to Rohemia with him. We're a tight-knit family, and I know that they will support me no matter what I ultimately decide, but I wouldn't feel right making this huge decision without hearing their opinions on the matter first. And since Kara, Charlotte, and Carly have always been like sisters to me—and they're always invited to spend the holidays with my family—I know that they'll tell me what they think about everything, too.

I pull into the driveway just in time to see my friends heading through the door, with my mom standing there waving at me excitedly. "Hey, Mom," I yell as I open my car door and step out into the snowy driveway.

"Hi, sweetie, come on in! I already have some cookies ready to be frosted, so wash your hands, and let's get to decorating!" I laugh at her enthusiasm before quickly making my way inside to get ready for a fun day of family traditions. After stopping at the kitchen sink to wash my hands, I turn towards the counter, tying an apron around my waist as I walk over to where everyone else is already waiting for me patiently.

"You're all smiles, Sarah. You must have had a good time over the last couple of days," my mom says. She already knows that I met someone the other day and that we've been spending time together—she just doesn't know *all* of the details— so her comment doesn't surprise me.

"The last couple of days have been—amazing, actually." I can't help the smile the spreads across my face as I think about all of the moments that Jeff and I have shared since I knocked him off of his feet, literally. Deciding that now is as good a time as any, I reach for a cookie and the jar of frosting before saying, "So—I have some news."

"What is it honey?" my mom asks while the rest of them look at me expectantly.

"Well, as you know, I've been spending time with Jeff since I met him on the ski hill."

"We know," says Kara, a playful smirk tugging at her lips.

I take a deep breath, bracing myself, as I prepare to tell them the rest of the news. "He and I spent the night together last night."

"That seems kind of fast," my dad says somewhat gruffly, his frosting spatula pausing midway to the cookie in his hand.

"I don't remember you waiting much longer when we first met, dear," my mom says with a soft chuckle.

"Eww—too much information!" I say, shaking my head, trying to get the unwanted image of my parents out of my mind. "Anyways, that's not the news. When we were talking afterwards last night, he made a confession to me. He's—well—it turns out that Jeff is actually a prince."

"A what?!" exclaim Charlotte and Kara together as they both look at me with their mouths hanging open comically, the cookies they were frosting momentarily forgotten.

"Yeah—right," says Carly in disbelief.

"No, really. He's the prince of Rohemia, a small country in Europe."

"Oh, my," says my mom.

"I know. I didn't believe it at first either." I reach towards the plate to grab another cookie to frost, taking a moment to gather my courage before continuing. "Before he left this morning, he asked me something. He told me that he would like it if I were to go back with him when he leaves so that we can continue to get to know each other some more."

"Go back with him?" Carly asks. "As in, to Europe? To—where is it—Rohemia?"

"Yes."

"And?" prompts my mom.

"And—I've decided that I want to go with him. I know that it seems completely crazy, but—" I shrug. "I don't know. I just feel like if I don't take this chance, then I'll regret it."

Mom's eyes lock onto mine—gentle, yet searching—as if she's trying to hear what my heart is saying, even if I haven't found the words to speak it. "You really care about this man don't you, Sarah?" she finally says without breaking eye contact.

"I do mom, I really do."

Mom and dad share a meaningful look before she turns to me again. "Then, we're happy for you. Just keep in touch and visit every now and then, okay?"

"I will. I promise."

"We're so excited for you, Sarah! You're dating a prince!" Charlotte and Kara shriek in unison, bubbling over with excitement.

"I may think that you're *completely* insane for

moving across the world with this man, but you have to do what you believe is right in your heart. Just be careful—you've only known him for a few days," Carly finally says.

"I will be, don't worry."

The rest of the day goes by quickly as I share all of the information that I know about Rohemia—and Jeff—since my parents and friends all want to know more about what I'm getting myself into. When evening finally rolls around, I head home to get ready for the parade before Jeff arrives to pick me up. I slip on a pair of my warmest wool socks along with my thermals beneath a pair of jeans and a thick sweatshirt with my ski jacket on top. Jeff arrives, looking as if he's dressed equally as warm, and I grin. "You were right, it's freezing out here tonight," he says as we walk to the car.

"I know. Sorry that I don't look cute tonight—I chose comfort and warmth over looks."

He laughs. "You look great. Honestly, I think that you'd look beautiful in anything."

I can't help the blush that stains my cheeks at his compliment. "Thanks."

A little while later we arrive in Ironwood, the small town already glowing with holiday lights and energy. We find a place to stand along the parade route, the air buzzing in anticipation, and the scent of food drifting into the street from the nearby diner. Once the parade starts, we watch as winter themed floats make their way down the street along with bands and dance troupes. Jeff holds me close, lending me a little extra warmth, as we watch dogs from the animal shelter walk by dressed in lighted hats, collars, and booties. The enormous snowmobile trail groomers—decorated with strings of twinkling lights and garlands—roll down the street, as well as the decorated firetrucks and tractors. Glancing over at Jeff, I know that he has never seen anything quite like this before, but he seems genuinely happy to be watching this parade with me. Turning my gaze back to the parade route, a feeling of joy fills me as I see all of the children around me watching—their eyes dancing—and cheering with glee as Santa Claus makes his appearance at the end of the parade lineup.

When the parade is finally over, we make our way inside Ben's Place, the small restaurant nearby, and sit down for some appetizers. "What was it like growing up as a prince?" I ask Jeff as we wait for our food.

"It had its advantages—and disadvantages. I had a loving family and all of the best schooling, I was never in need of anything, and the palace was like a huge playground for me. But growing up royal also meant that I had to meet certain—expectations, and people always treated me differently."

"That has to be rough."

"It was, and it still is, but at least I've always had Nigel. He's always been there for me as a friend when I've needed him."

"How did you two meet?"

"His parents worked for my parents, so we kind of grew up together. Then, when we were older, he became my bodyguard as well as my friend."

Jeff patiently answers all of my questions, and tells me about his life in Rohemia while we share cheese curds and deep fried pickles—two foods that he had never eaten before tonight, but has now added to his list of favorites. "These are sooo good. I don't usually eat fried foods very often, but I think that once I get back to Rohemia, I'm going to have to introduce these to our chef at the palace."

I laugh. "I'm sure that he—or she?—will love that."

"He—and yes, I think that he will actually. He likes to shake things up every now and then."

"I'll find a recipe for both of them for you."

"Thanks. That would be nice."

After we're finished eating, he drives us back to my house and joins me inside. "Would you mind lighting a fire in the fireplace while I pour us both a glass of wine, please?" I ask. "There's something that I want to talk to you about."

"Sure, of course."

He gets to work on that while I excuse myself to the kitchen, returning a few moments later with two glasses of Chardonnay. Once we're both settled on the couch, he takes my hand in his and asks, "Is everything alright? What did you want to talk about?"

I take a small sip before turning to look him in the eyes. "Jeff, I've thought a lot about what you asked me this morning, and I talked it over with my family and friends. I've made a decision. When you go back to Rohemia, I'll come with you."

His eyes light up, glowing with happiness and a flicker of hope. "Are you sure?" he asks, searching my face. "If you need more time—"

"I don't. I've never been more sure of anything in my entire life."

He leans in slowly, and when our lips meet, the kiss is long and tender—sweet, yet laced with unde-niable passion. "Hearing you say that makes me the happiest man in the world."

"I could add to that happiness," I say, a wicked smirk tugging at my lips.

"Oh, yeah? What did you have in mind?" he asks with a knowing grin.

We spend the rest of the night making passionate love to one another in front of the fire-place, cuddling in each others arms in between rounds, surrounded by the warm glow of the fire and the twinkling Christmas tree in the background. It makes me even more certain that my decision to go with Jeff is the right one.

Jeff

Over the next week, Sarah and I spend time packing up her belongings and making the necessary arrangements for her to join me in Rohemia. The plan is for her to stay with me for six months so that we have adequate time to learn more about each other, but if all goes well, I hope that she'll make the move permanent.

We're in the process of packing the last of the items that she wants to bring with her when I finally broach the topic of my conversation that I had with my parents. "I finally spoke to my parents last night."

"You did? What did they say? Am I packing for no reason?" she asks nervously.

"No, of course not—you're still coming with

me. They were a little surprised when I told them that I was bringing my new girlfriend home with me, but overall they took it pretty well, I think. They have agreed to have a room prepared for you at the palace."

"The palace—I don't know if I'll ever get used to that. But I look forward to meeting the King and Queen. I hope that they find me—acceptable," Sarah says a little sheepishly. "Are you sure that they're okay with me staying there? I don't want to impose on royalty."

"Don't worry—you're the woman that I love, so you'll never be an imposition. Besides, my parents will love you, and it'll be great for you to experience what life in the palace is like," I say, comforting her.

"I hope that you're right." She hesitates, pulling her bottom lip between her teeth, chewing on it nervously for a second before continuing. "The fact that I'm the woman that you love, and I'm *not* royal, is what worries me. I've watched all of the royal romance movies—the King and Queen are never happy about the idea of their heir being with a commoner."

Laughter bubbles up from my chest, and I'm unable to hold it in. I pull her into my arms, hugging her tightly against my chest as I kiss her softly. When I pull back, I reassure her that she has nothing to worry about. "Relax, Sarah. My parents are nothing like the royals that you see in the movies. They don't believe in the whole arranged marriage, keeping the bloodline pure thing. They've always taught me that I'm free to follow my heart as long as I don't neglect my royal responsibilities— and the woman who will one day reign at my side can be whoever I choose her to be."

She meets my eyes for a moment, and all I see is hope reflected back at me. "Really?"

"Yes, really. I never would have pursued you if I was forbidden from marrying outside of nobility. Not because I wouldn't have been interested in you, but because ultimately you would have been hurt in the end, and I would never do that to you."

She brushes her lips against mine before nodding. "I know that you wouldn't. And knowing what I do now about your parents, that makes me feel a little bit better at least. I really am looking forward to meeting them and staying at the palace with you." She pulls out of my arms to return to her packing, folding another sweater and placing it into her suitcase. "Well, that's the last shirt that I needed to pack." She zips up her bag and places it on the floor.

"Good. Are you all ready, then?"

"I think so. All that's left now is to enjoy the holidays with my family and friends, and say our goodbyes. Speaking of which, Christmas Eve is in a few days, and my parents have invited you to spend it with us at their home."

"That sounds wonderful—though I'm still a little worried about how they'll react to having me there since I'm taking their only daughter away."

"Don't be silly—they're the ones who extended the invite. They're okay with the fact that I'm going to Europe with you. Really. They just want to officially meet you before I do."

"Well, then, I'm looking forward to spending time with them as well." I smile and wrap my arms around her waist. "Until it's time to leave for Rohemia, I want nothing more than to be wherever you are."

"I think that can be arranged," Sarah says as she leans up to kiss me again. "There's still a few more days for me to show you the rest of the holiday festivities that Bessemer has to offer—along with a few special, festive, activities of my own to show you," she adds with a gleam in her eye.

I'm not sure what she has in store for me, but I like the sound of *that*.

When Sarah and I arrive at her parents' home on Christmas Eve, her parents are waiting for us at the door. "Thank you for inviting me this evening," I say a little nervously. Even though Sarah has reassured me that they're okay with everything, I'm still anxious around them.

"Of course! We couldn't let you spend Christmas alone—especially if you're dating our daughter," her mother says cheerfully as she takes the gifts that we brought and heads into the living room to put them under the tree.

"We've had the privilege of getting to know you over the past couple of days—and Sarah talks about you so much—it feels like you're already part of our family, son," her father adds as he pats me on the back.

"Well, thank you for trusting me enough to take your daughter halfway around the world with me."

"We trust *you* because Sarah trusts you—but if you break her heart or hurt her in any way, I *will* hunt you down," he warns. "I don't care if you *are* a prince."

Sarah throws her hands in the air, her eyes wide with exaggerated exasperation. "Dad!"

I throw my head back, loud laughter escaping me as my shoulders shake. "It's okay, Sarah. I like that your father speaks his mind—and don't worry, Sir, I promise that I'll take good care of her."

"Good man," he says.

"Okay, now that we have that out of the way, let's sit down to eat before the food gets cold," her mother says as she returns from the living room, shaking her head.

We all follow her into the dining room, where the glow of twinkling lights from a garland strung up around the window adds a soft warmth to the room. The table is a holiday masterpiece— completely covered in large serving platters and festive bowls, each one overflowing with something delicious. At the center sits a magnificent Christmas ham, its brown sugar glaze caramelized to perfection and topped with golden pineapple rings and maraschino cherries, like ornaments on a holiday roast.

Around it, the table is packed with holiday favorites like creamy mashed potatoes topped with a melting pat of butter, baked beans with a hint of molasses, and a deep bowl of green bean casserole, topped with a layer of french-fried onions. A cranberry salad sparkles like rubies in a crystal dish, and a basket of warm dinner rolls wrapped in a red cloth steams gently in the corner. Tucked between the classics are dishes filled with deviled eggs topped with paprika, buttered corn, and a warm lemon meringue pie. The whole room smells like Christmas. "It smells wonderful in here!" Sarah says excitedly.

"This dinner looks lovely, Mrs. Duncan," I add.

"Thank you, Jeff."

We all gather around the table, laughter and chatter already filling the air as we settle in to enjoy the Christmas feast. Plates are passed around, everyone dishing up their plates, and the sound of silverware clinking against porcelain is the only noise for a few minutes as we enjoy our first couple of bites. The room is humming with warmth, happiness, and the unmistakable comfort of family, and I feel surrounded by love. I can't help but think about how blessed I am to be able to share in this holiday experience with Sarah and her parents, especially since I'm away from my own family this holiday season. Even though I've always felt burdened with obligations during the holidays back home, my parents and I still celebrated Christmas together, so it's nice to still be surrounded with people I care about since my own family isn't here.

Once the last crumb has been eaten, the table cleared, and the leftovers neatly packed away, we drift into the living room, feeling full and content. The glow of the Christmas tree greets us, its twinkling lights casting soft reflections on the windows and sparkling off of the ornaments and shiny garlands. Sarah's father moves to the corner and clicks on the stereo, and within moments, the room fills with the gentle sound of holiday classics—songs that we've all heard thousands of times, but never tire of. We sink into the couches and armchairs, enjoying the peaceful moment together.

After a few moments, her father gets up again, pulling two beautifully wrapped presents out from underneath the Christmas tree. "We wanted to get you both something before you leave," he says. He hands one package to me and the other to Sarah.

"Oh my gosh! I love it!" Sarah exclaims as she rips through the wrapping paper and pulls a fancy floor-length gown from the package. "Thank you!" She throws her arms around each of her parents to give them both a hug.

"We thought that you could use a new dress—

you know, in case there are any fancy balls at the palace," her mother says.

I look at Sarah. Her excitement is contagious, and I find myself smiling, drawn in by the joy dancing in her eyes. "We'll have a special ball just for us if there aren't any planned."

"Promise?" she asks.

"Promise."

She laughs happily. "Good—now open yours."

I turn the package around in my hands to find the end of the wrapping paper. "You didn't have to get me anything," I say as I begin to unwrap the present.

"We wanted to," her father says. "It's not much, but we wanted you to have a souvenir from the U.P."

I pull the paper away to reveal a sweatshirt emblazoned with the outline of the Upper Penin-sula and a slogan—*Say yah to da U.P., eh!*—that I've seen many times since I arrived here. I chuckle softly, tugging it over my head with a grin. "What do you think?" I ask.

"It looks great on you," Sarah says.

I turn to her parents. "Thank you. I'll wear it often."

"You're welcome," they reply in unison.

"Okay, my turn!" Sarah says. She retrieves the gifts that she bought from under the tree, passing them out to everyone. Her dad is thrilled with his curated whiskey set—complete with a 'Best Dad Ever' glass—and her mom has tears in her eyes when she opens the pearl necklace and earring set that Sarah bought for her.

When it's my turn, I carefully unwrap the small box in front of me. As soon as the paper is removed, my breath catches. In a deep, wooden frame—set behind glass—are several meaningful items. A ski lift ticket from Indianhead with the date that Sarah and I met stamped on it, the small booklet of Christmas carols that we used on the sleigh ride, a receipt from El Tarasco where we had our first date, and a picture of us together at the Jack Frost Parade. "It's a memory box," she says. "I wasn't sure what else to get you."

I wrap my arms around her, hugging her tightly, and my voice wavers slightly when I answer. "This is perfect, Sarah. I love it. Thank you."

"You're welcome."

"My turn. Forgive me, but I think that my gift to you will pale in comparison to the gift that you gave me."

"I highly doubt that," she scoffs. "I'll love anything that you give me."

I smile, handing her a small, green and silver wrapped box. "I saw this in a store window when I went out a few days ago, and it reminded me of you. I hope that you like it."

She tears the paper away, revealing the black velvet box that I know contains a charm bracelet, adorned with several charms—a pair of skis, a sleigh, and a snowflake. "Oh, Jeff," she gasps, tears in her eyes. "I love it." She quickly brushes her lips against mine, and wipes the tears from her cheeks. "I told you that it wouldn't be any less special than what I gave you," she says as I clasp the bracelet around her wrist.

Her parents watch us with warm smiles, and when our eyes meet, they each give me a subtle nod of approval. The gesture settles something inside of me—reassurance that they truly support Sarah's decision to move with me. Grateful, I turn my attention towards them, wanting them to see just how much that means to me. "I have one more gift to give." I find the gift that I brought for them under the tree and hand it to her parents. "It's just a little something that I'd like for you both to have," I say as I hand it to her mother.

She delicately removes the bow, placing it to the side before tearing at the wrapping paper. Opening the lid of the wooden box inside, her eyes go wide as she gazes down into it. "It's beautiful!" she exclaims, carefully lifting the handcrafted ornament from the box—a delicate partridge nestled in a pear tree. I smile as she and Sarah's dad lean in to admire it together, their fingers gently brushing over the intricate carving and the stunningly detailed paintwork—the feathers, the leaves, even the tiny golden pears, all brought to life with remarkable care.

"I hope that you like it. It's a family heirloom—I brought it to Michigan with me so that I could have a little piece of home on my tree while I'm here, but it's yours now."

"Oh, we couldn't!" her mother says, eyes wide as she looks from me to the ornament. "It's a family heirloom—a *royal* family heirloom."

Her father nods in agreement, his tone gentle but firm. "That's far too generous. We couldn't possibly accept something so valuable."

"Please," I say, smiling softly. "I want you to have it. This ornament has been passed down in my family for generations, but it has always been meant to be passed on to someone who has earned our trust and our gratitude. Both of you have done that. And you've shown me love this Christmas season—you've welcomed me into your home, allowed me to be a part of your family traditions, and the greatest gift of all—you're trusting me to be with your daughter."

They glance at each other, both visibly moved. Her mother's hand moves to her chest and her eyes are misty. "Are you sure? This is no small gesture."

"I'm positive. Your daughter means the world to me, and welcoming me into your home the way that you have—it means more to me than I can ever say."

"Thank you," she says as she gives me a hug.

Her father places his hand on my shoulder, clearing his throat. "Thank you. We'll treasure it—not because it's royal, but because it's from you."

"You're welcome."

The weight of the moment settles warmly between us, emotion shimmering in everyone's eyes—including Sarah's as she reaches for my hand, smiling up at me with a soft, grateful smile. "That was very sweet of you," she whispers as we settle back onto the couch. "And I think that you just made me fall even more in love with you than I already was."

I wrap my arm around her shoulders, tucking her more snuggly into my side and kissing the top of her head as her mother passes around mugs of hot chocolate. "I love you, too," I whisper as everyone cuddles up with warm blankets, settling in to watch Christmas movies for the rest of the night. As I look around the living room at the people surrounding me—experiencing another one of Sarah's family traditions—I smile to myself. There's no doubt about it, this has been the best holiday that I've had in a long time.

Sarah

On Christmas Day, I drive over to Jeff's chalet bright and early, with my parents and the girls tagging along. Jeff graciously invited everyone over so that we can share one last gathering before he and I leave for Rohemia—a chance to spend the holiday together, all under one roof. When we arrive, he opens the door with a smile lighting up his face. "Merry Christmas, everyone! Come on in."

"Thank you for having all of us," my mom says.

"You're welcome. After the wonderful celebration that we had last night, I wanted to return the favor. Besides, I want Sarah to spend as much time with all of you as she can before we leave."

We all follow him into the living room, and as

we make ourselves comfortable, Nigel enters from the kitchen carrying a tray of hors d'oeuvres. "Hi, Nigel. It's good to see you again," I say.

"It's good to see you again, too, Miss Duncan."

I chuckle. "No need to be so formal—please, call me Sarah."

"Good luck with that," Jeff says with a smirk.

Nigel gives me a small smile. "I'll try my best—but being so formal is a hard habit for me to break."

"I guess that's understandable considering your profession. But I insist."

"Alright. Sarah."

"Hey! I've been trying to get you to call me just plain old Jeff the entire time that we've been here," Jeff grumbles with an exaggerated pout, drawing laughter from all of us.

I grin and stick out my tongue. "Yes, but I'm not royalty, I really *am* just plain old Sarah." He looks like he's about to say something in protest, but I quickly continue. "Are you preparing all of the food, Nigel?" I ask curiously.

"No, actually. *Jeff,*" he says, drawing out his name with playful emphasis, "has prepared most of it. I just made the hors d'oeuvres."

I look over at Jeff and raise my eyebrows. "So—the prince knows how to cook, huh?"

He chuckles. "I do. And I didn't think that it was fair to make Nigel do all of the work on Christmas—especially when I was the one who invited the extra guests." I smile to myself at his admission. The way that he stays so grounded—never arrogant, never playing the royalty card—makes me love him even more.

We all enjoy munching on the tasty little snacks that Nigel made while we wait for the main course to be served. As usual, laughter and cheerful chatter fill the air, wrapping us in joyful energy as we sit gathered in the living room, talking. As soon as the meal is ready, Jeff leads us into the dining room, presenting the wonderful feast that he has prepared —a traditional Rohemian casserole filled with meat, mashed potatoes, and a creamy Béchamel sauce; as well as a couple of American side dishes, and Christmas cookies for dessert.

"I know that it's not as grand of a feast as we had last night, but I hope that this will suffice," Jeff says as he pulls out my chair.

"It's plenty. Thank you for cooking for all of us."

"It was my pleasure. It's been a while since I've cooked for anyone besides myself, honestly, and I enjoyed it."

"Well, it looks yummy!" Kara says.

"Smells good, too," adds Charlotte.

"Thank you. Everyone, help yourselves."

We pass around the dishes, scooping a little of everything onto our plates before digging in. When the first bite hits my tongue, I let out a little moan of satisfaction, causing Jeff's eyes to darken. He gently squeezes my knee under the table, leaning down to whisper into my ear. "If you keep making noises like that at the dinner table, I can't promise that I'll be able to keep myself from doing something inappropriate in front of your parents and friends."

"Sorry," I whisper back. "It just tastes *so* good!"

He chuckles. "I'm glad that you like it."

The girls send knowing glances at me from across the table, smirking and lifting their eyebrows. "This tastes delicious, doesn't it everyone?" I ask, trying to distract their attention away from Jeff and I.

"Yes, it's excellent. Thank you, Jeff," my mom says.

"You're welcome."

Once we're all finished eating and everything has been cleaned up, we alternate playing board games and telling stories about our best Christmas memories. Even Nigel participates. More gifts are exchanged—with the girls and Nigel this time—and at the end of the night some tears are shed, knowing that I leave first thing tomorrow morning.

My parents and the girls say their goodbyes to Jeff and Nigel before waving and making their way out to the car. I hang back at the door, my arms wrapped around Jeff's waist. "I'm sorry that I'm not staying with you tonight," I say as I kiss him softly. "Especially since I—maybe—turned you on a little at dinner."

"You *definitely* turned me on at dinner," he says with a chuckle. "But I'll be fine. I understand that you need to spend one final night with your family before we leave."

I nod. "Yeah, I do. I'll make it up to you, I promise."

"I'll hold you to that," he says with a smirk. "I'll pick you up bright and early tomorrow, okay?"

"Okay, I'll see you tomorrow. Thanks for one of the best Christmases that I've ever had." I brush my lips against his once more before waving goodbye and walking out to join everyone else in my car.

I spend the night tossing and turning, caught somewhere between excitement and nerves, unable to settle into sleep. By the time that Jeff pulls up to my parents' house, I'm already by the door, ready and waiting.

"Are you ready?" he asks as he and Nigel walk up to retrieve my bags.

I take a deep breath, my heart fluttering, and nod with a smile. "Ready as I'll ever be." With one last hug and a lingering goodbye to my parents, I turn towards Jeff, letting him take my hand as he whisks me away to a new life—one filled with unknowns, adventure, and most importantly, him.

Sarah

❦

A s our private jet touches down in Rohemia twelve hours later, the nervousness that has plagued me occasionally ever since I first began thinking about meeting Jeff's parents—the King and Queen—returns. The anxiety that I'm feeling must show on my face because Jeff squeezes my hand reassuringly. "You have nothing to worry about, Sarah. They'll love you."

"You're sure?"

"I'm positive." He pulls me into his embrace, kissing me softly before releasing me. "As soon as you meet my parents, you'll see that they're nothing like the royals that you've seen on TV."

"Okay." I smile at him, deciding to trust in the fact that he knows his parents' wishes.

The jet finally comes to a complete stop inside the hangar, and Nigel informs us that there is already a car waiting to take us to the palace. "I'll get your bags for you and meet you at the car, Your Highness. Miss Duncan, I'll grab yours as well."

"Really, Nigel? Back to formalities? I thought that we had moved past that," I tease.

He gives me a slight grin. "Yes, Miss Duncan— we *had* moved past that. But that was when we were celebrating Christmas in a ski chalet in Michigan. We're in Rohemia now, and you're a guest of His Royal Highness, not to mention Their Majesties, the King and Queen."

"Oh. Of—of course," I stutter. "Forgive me. I should have thought of that."

"Don't worry, Miss Duncan. I know that you're not familiar with royal protocol yet."

I glance over at Jeff nervously while Nigel goes to retrieve our belongings. "I'm going to make a total fool out of myself, aren't I?"

He chuckles as he wraps an arm around my shoulders. "Relax. You're not going to make a fool out of yourself. I'd never let that happen. I'll teach you what you need to know if it's necessary."

"Do I need to address you as 'Your Highness' now? And what about your parents?"

He looks at me lovingly, giving me a patient smile. "If we're in public, or at a social event, then yes—as part of protocol, you'll have to address me as 'Your Highness'. My parents you address as 'Your Majesties'. But if we're in the privacy of the palace, I'm just plain old Jeff—and you can drop the formal titles for my parents as well."

"You're sure that's okay? But Nigel said—"

"Yes, I know. But Nigel—even though he's one of my best friends—is still one of my employees. He's had formality ingrained in him since birth. And as he said—*you* are my guest." He tilts my chin up so that I'm looking into his eyes. "Okay?"

I nod. "Okay."

"Good. Now, let's go to the car before he comes looking for us."

I let Jeff lead me off of the jet, out into the hangar, and to the waiting limousine. Once we're both inside, the driver slowly pulls out, beginning the drive towards the palace. Jeff holds my hand, his thumb gently stroking against the back of it, as he tells me about all of the landmarks that we're passing. I gaze out the window excitedly, taking in all of the sights around me. From what I've seen of it so far, Rohemia truly is breathtaking.

As the car begins the trek up a winding path,

Jeff directs my attention to the front. My eyes instantly widen and my jaw drops at what I see before me. Looming over the countryside, at the end of the path, sits a genuine Victorian castle. Contrary to what he's told me—about his parents at least—the palace really does remind me of all of the castles that I've seen in movies and in story-books. It's massive, with towering turrets, pointed arches, and surrounded by a stunning walled garden. "Wow," I whisper. "This is incredible."

"Welcome to my home, Sarah."

I'm still trying to process everything that I'm seeing when the car pulls to a stop in front of the grand palace. Nigel opens the door, and Jeff steps out before taking my hand, helping me to crawl out behind him. We climb the front steps, and when we reach the top, he stops, wrapping his arms around my waist and pulling me against his chest. He leans his forehead against mine—a gesture that has become comforting to me—and gives me a slow, tender kiss. "Remember—I love you, and my parents will, too. Just breathe."

I nod my head before whispering, "Thank you."

The doors are opened for us by armed guards, who up until now have reminded me of stone statues—standing completely still and silent on either side of the large double doors. Jeff nods in thanks before leading me inside. My eyes quickly scan my surroundings, trying to take in all of the luxuriousness as I follow him down a long hallway. "Where are we going?"

"To introduce you to my parents." He glances over at me, smirking at the look of pure panic on my face. "I figured that it would be best to get it out of the way now instead of waiting. Otherwise, I have a feeling that you'll be a nervous wreck all day waiting to meet them at dinner."

I laugh nervously. "You're probably right."

When we reach another set of double doors at the end of the hall, Jeff knocks once before entering the spacious parlor, gently tugging me in behind him. "Mother, Father. I'm home."

"Jeff! Oh, I missed you!" his mother exclaims as she rushes over to hug him. "How was your Christmas?"

"It was wonderful."

"Was it everything that you were hoping for when you decided to take your little adventure?" his father asks, smiling as he steps up to take his turn hugging him.

"Yes, and then some," Jeff says, smiling happily

as he turns his gaze back to me. "Mother, Father—I'd like you to meet Sarah, my girlfriend."

The King and Queen both turn their attention towards me as I awkwardly attempt to curtsey. "Your Majesties, it's a pleasure to meet you both."

The Queen reaches out to take my hand, gently urging me to stand. "Come, now, Sarah. There's no need for you to be so formal with us here. You can call me Eleanor, and this is my husband, James."

"It's very nice to finally meet you, Sarah. Our son has spoken very highly of you," the King says kindly. "Please, come sit. Join us for tea."

"Thank you," I say, a genuine smile lighting up my face. Jeff was right—his parents are nothing like what I was expecting. They both appear to be very accepting of my relationship with him—at least so far.

"Did you have a good flight?" his mother asks as she offers me a cup of tea.

"Oh, yes. The jet was amazing. I've never flown in anything so comfortable before."

"It was a very relaxing, uneventful flight," Jeff adds.

"Well, that's good to hear. Once we're finished with tea, Jeff, you can show Sarah to her room. We've had the one next to yours prepared for her."

"Alright." We all drink our tea, chatting as his parents get to know me better, asking questions about my life in Michigan and what my family is like. "Is there anything else that you need me to take care of before dinner since I've been gone?" Jeff finally asks.

"Yes, actually. There are a few things that I need to go over with you. Just come see me in my office after you bring Sarah to her room. No rush, of course," his father says.

He nods as he finishes the last sip of his tea. "Sarah, are you ready? Nigel should have your belongings in your room by now."

"Yes, I'm ready." I set my teacup down and stand up. "Eleanor, James—thank you again for allowing me to stay at the palace." It feels strange addressing them so informally, but who am I to argue with their request.

"Of course, dear," Jeff's mother says with a smile. "As long as you're with our son, you'll always be welcome here."

I take Jeff's offered hand and follow him back out into the hallway. As he leads me up a set of stairs, he says, "There, that wasn't so bad, was it?"

I shake my head. "No, not at all. Your parents

were both very welcoming—and not at all what I was expecting from royalty."

"See, I told you that they would love you," he says with a grin. When we reach the third floor, he opens a door that leads to the most beautiful bedroom that I've ever seen. "Welcome to your room."

My eyes roam around the spacious bedroom. White and gray marble floors shine under the light of the large crystal chandelier. A plush, blue velvet sofa and matching armchairs surround a Mahogany coffee table in the sitting area, and a luxurious king-sized bed sits on the other side of the room, covered in fluffy pillows and draped by a gold silk canopy. "This is just—wow. I actually get to stay here?" I ask, turning towards Jeff, my eyes wide with awe.

"Yes, you really do," he says with a laugh as he pulls me into his arms. His lips meet mine, kissing me softly for a moment before his tongue slips into my mouth. Our tongues tangle together, and I whimper as his hands find their way into my hair. We kiss for another minute before he finally pulls away. "As much as I want to keep going, duty calls. I need to go meet with my father, and you need to get settled in before dinner. *But*, later—we're going to pick up where we left off."

"Okay," I say a little breathlessly.

"I'll be back at six to escort you to dinner. In the meantime, if you need anything just push that call button over there on the wall, and Nigel will come to assist you."

"Sounds good." He turns to leave, but I call out to stop him. "Jeff? Just one more question."

"What is it?"

"What on earth do I wear to dinner?"

A laugh escapes his lips as he shakes his head. "Just wear what you normally would for dinner."

I put my hands on my hips and raise my eyebrows. "What I would normally wear is leggings and a sweater or jeans and a hoodie."

He shrugs. "Either one is fine. I told you—when it's just us at the palace, everything is pretty laid-back and informal. I promise—my parents won't be offended no matter what you wear."

"Okay, if you say so."

"I do. And you should know by now that I'm always right." He winks at me before stepping out into the hall, closing the door behind him.

I chuckle to myself, shaking my head. As much as I want to argue that I should wear something fancier for dinner with the King and Queen, Jeff—so far—*has* always been right.

Jeff

Since arriving back in Rohemia earlier today, time seems to have flown by. After introducing Sarah to my parents this afternoon and taking care of some official business with my father, we ate a lovely dinner with them and visited until they decided to turn in for the evening. Now, Sarah and I are making our way back to her room. "You look beautiful tonight, by the way," I say, glancing at her out of the corner of my eye.

"Thank you. I'm glad that I decided to listen to you and went with leggings and my favorite red sweater. Otherwise, I would have been over-dressed."

I laugh. "Yes, you would have been. Don't

worry—I'll let you know when more formal attire is expected."

"Thank you. This is all so new to me, and it's difficult trying to reconcile the reality with what I've always pictured."

"It's not always like this. A lot of the time, it *is* like what you were expecting, but when it's just us here—we get to be a normal family. Or at least act like one."

"With a butler, and a chef, and a maid. Oh! And don't forget about the guards," Sarah says cheekily, smirking at me.

"Yes, well—that can't be helped," I say with a laugh as I come to a stop outside of her bedroom door. Turning the handle, I push the door open, motioning for her to enter first. "After you."

She makes her way into the room, and I follow her, pushing the door closed behind me until the lock softly clicks into place. My hands instantly find her hips, pulling her towards me. "Now, where were we earlier?" I ask as my mouth hungrily searches for hers.

"Right about here." Her arms wrap around my neck, her body pressing tightly against mine. One of my hands trails slowly upwards, under her sweater, leaving a trail of goosebumps in its wake.

When I finally cup her breast, my fingertips brushing against her lacy bra-covered nipple, she gasps, tearing her lips from mine. "Jeff, we should stop."

"You want me to stop?" I ask, kissing and nipping my way down her neck.

She shakes her head. "No. No, I don't *want* you to. But we should. Your parents—"

"I assure you, my parents don't care." My lips continue exploring as my fingers lightly pinch her nipple, making her moan.

"But—"

"No buts. The only reason that you have your own room is for the illusion of propriety's sake—and so that you can have some privacy when you want it. My parents aren't naive—they've guessed that we're already sleeping together. Why do you think that they gave you the room next to mine?"

My hand works its way into her leggings, under her panties, and my fingers slowly begin playing with her clit. "Oh, fuuuuck. I've been wanting your touch for days. Don't stop," she begs.

"I won't, but let's make this a little easier, shall we? Wrap your legs around my waist." I move my hand out of the way so that she can do what I've asked, and then carry her over to the bed, setting her down gently. "There, that's better. Lie back." I gently push her backwards until she's flat on her back before tugging off her leggings and panties. "I've wanted to taste you ever since hearing those noises that you were making during Christmas dinner." I sink to my knees in front of her, burying my face between her legs.

"Ohhhh, yes!" she moans as my tongue flicks against her clit before trailing up and down her core. As I move my tongue back towards her clit, I slip one finger inside, pumping in a slow, steady rhythm. Keeping the pressure on her bundle of nerves light, I alternate circling it and flicking my tongue up and down. When her hands try to hold my head in place, I add a second finger to her entrance, pumping a little faster, while continuing the rhythm that I have with my tongue. "Jeff, please."

I smile against her center. "You like that, baby?" I ask, chuckling at her groan of displeasure at the loss of contact on her clit from my tongue.

"Please, don't stop. I'm so close." My mouth resumes its previous ministrations while my fingers continue pumping in and out of her, curling just slightly to hit that spot inside of her. When I finally suck her clit into my mouth, she comes undone, trembling as she shouts my name with her release.

Wiping my mouth with the back of my hand, I stand up, tugging my pants and boxers off in the process. As I climb onto the bed, my hand strokes along my cock, once, twice, smearing the bead of pre-cum over the tip. Sarah watches me with heavy-lidded eyes. "Do you want me?" I ask.

"Mmm-hmm," she says with a nod.

"How do you want me?"

"I don't care, as long as you're inside of me."

"Come here, then." Standing back up, I gently pull her closer to the edge of the bed until only her head and back are still touching. Draping her legs on either side of my hips, I push my cock into her entrance until I'm sheathed fully inside. "Fuck, you feel good." Slowly, I pull back out before sliding back in, twisting my hips a bit at the end.

I can feel her walls tightening, squeezing me more and more with each thrust. As I lift one of her legs into the air, resting it on my shoulder—and deepening the angle—we both moan at the new sensation. My legs begin to tremble, and I let my head fall backwards, my eyes closing, as I feel my control slipping. I thrust into her, harder, faster, each time my movements becoming a bit more erratic.

Bringing my thumb to her clit, I begin circling it, adding a little more pressure each time that my cock slides into her. With a few more rocks of my hips, she topples over the edge, and a second later I'm following, moaning with my own release.

We're both breathless as we collapse into a sweaty heap in bed a minute later, wrapped in each other's arms. She rests her head on my chest, her fingers idly tracing along my muscles. "Thank you for talking me into doing that. It was amazing."

I chuckle. "It didn't take that much convincing."

She laughs. "No, you're right, it didn't. But still. I wasn't sure how your parents would feel about us sleeping together under the palace roof. Especially when they've only just met me."

"We're both adults. And we love each other. That's all that matters."

She kisses my chest. "I do love you."

"I know. And I love you."

Epilogue

SARAH

One year later…..

The soft strains of music drift through the palace, growing clearer with each step that I take towards the grand ballroom. The long hallway is a vision of holiday splendor—lined with towering Christmas trees, each one uniquely decorated with shimmering gold ornaments; twinkling lights that cast a warm, enchanting glow along the marble floors; and dusted with powdery, white, artificial snow. The scent of pine and something faintly spiced hangs in the air, wrapping around me like the winter magic that I remember from back home.

I feel exceptionally beautiful in the flowing purple gown—a strapless, A-line dress that flares out at the bottom, embellished with sequins and glitter along the bodice—that my parents gifted me last Christmas, and a stole of matching purple silk that's draped delicately around my arms. It's paired with a sparkling diamond necklace and tiara that the Queen let me borrow for tonight. Although I was nervous about meeting her last year, she and I have become surprisingly close. The same goes for the King—we get along remarkably well.

When I near the ballroom, I see Jeff waiting for me in the doorway, decked out in all of his royal attire. "Hello, your Highness," I say as I lower myself into a practiced curtsy, my eyes never leaving his.

"Hello, my love," he says as he takes my hand, bringing it to his lips for a gentle kiss. "Before we join the party, there's something that I want to give to you."

"What is it?"

"Come with me."

"Okay," I say, laughing as he tugs me along behind him, like an excited little kid on Christmas morning.

When we reach a set of double doors off to the side, he gently pulls me through onto a large moonlit balcony that overlooks the sea and the gardens below before closing the door behind us with a quiet click. I only have a couple of seconds to admire the view—the garden looks absolutely enchanted with the way that shimmering lights adorn the pathways, making the snow on the winter plants look like everything is covered in diamonds— before he turns towards me, his eyes meeting mine for only a heartbeat before he slips his arms around my waist and draws me into a kiss—deep, urgent, and filled with passion. By the time that we finally pull apart, we're both breathing heavily. He leans his forehead against mine and closes his eyes. "Sorry—I couldn't help myself. You look absolutely stunning."

"That's alright. But, here," I swipe my thumb across his lips, "you have a little lipstick smudged on you."

He chuckles. "Thanks. That might not go over so well once we go back out there."

"Probably not."

He clears his throat, a hint of nerves in his voice now. "Back to the real reason that I pulled you out here—there's something that I want to give you. Something that I've been wanting to give to you ever since we first met." Reaching into his pocket, he pulls out a small, blue velvet box. My breath catches as he opens it and drops to one knee. "You're the missing piece that I've been searching for. You complete me, Sarah. I knew from the second that I heard you laugh in the ski chalet, and saw your face, that I was in love with you. The past year has been the *absolute* best year of my life. You've proven that you love me for who I am in *here*," he says putting his hand over his heart, "and I love you more than anything else in the world. I can't imagine my life without you. Will you accept this ring and become my wife—and my princess?"

Tears fill my eyes, spilling down my cheeks as I nod happily. "Yes! Yes, a thousand times yes!" He slides the gorgeous ring onto my finger, before standing again, wrapping me in his arms once more, and giving me another kiss. This time there's nothing urgent about it—it's just one of his slow, passionate kisses that I love so much—and he's pouring every ounce of his love for me into it, not caring about smudged lipstick anymore.

When we finally come up for air, he releases me

from his embrace and holds an arm out for me to hold. Once we've both collected ourselves, he says, "Shall we? I'd like to show off my beautiful bride-to-be to the whole kingdom."

I laugh as I wrap my arm through his. "Let's."

As we make our way through the door of the grand ballroom a minute later to open the dancing portion of the evening, I gaze around the room, expecting to see the familiar faces of people that I've met during my time here in Rohemia along with some that I don't know, but what I'm not expecting is to see Charlotte, Kara, Carly, and my parents all fabulously dressed and waiting for us along with the rest of the guests. I look up at Jeff, my eyes dancing with excitement and joy, and he whispers, "I couldn't let you celebrate Christmas without *all* of your loved ones here." I squeeze his arm in thanks as I walk proudly by his side, knowing that I was wrong last year. *This* is the best Christmas that I've ever had.

Jeff

. . .

Sarah and I walk towards the center of the ballroom dance floor as the music changes to a slow holiday waltz. I take her in my arms, and we begin to perform the steps as everyone stands around in a circle, watching us. My eyes stay locked on hers as we slowly move across the floor, a smile plastered on both of our faces, and it's as if everyone else in the room disappears. My heart is full knowing that I get to spend the rest of my life dancing with this woman.

"The ring is beautiful by the way," Sarah says as I spin her in my arms.

"I'm glad that you like it—it belonged to my grandmother."

"Really? So it's a royal family heirloom?"

"It is. My mother gave it to me a while ago— not long after she met you. She said that she could tell that you were my soulmate from the moment that I introduced you to her and my father."

Sarah gazes at me, her smile full of affection. "I'm glad that I've got their approval to marry you. Even though you told me a long time ago that they were okay with you choosing your future wife, I was still a little bit worried that they would tell me that it was against royal tradition to marry a commoner or something."

"Well, it's true—regardless of their opinions on the matter, it's not usually done—but they would never stand in the way of true love."

The song ends, and we slowly make our way over to greet her family and friends. As soon as we're close enough to where they're standing, Sarah rushes over to hug all of them excitedly. "I've missed you guys so much!" she says through happy tears.

"We've missed you, too, sweetie," says her father as he pulls her into a hug.

"You look so royal!" gushes Kara when it's her turn.

"Thanks! I feel royal." She steals a quick glance in my direction, her lips curling into a secretive smile meant just for me, knowing that soon she *will* be royal.

While Sarah continues to catch up with her loved ones, my mother and father walk up beside me. "Congratulations, son," the King says. "Whenever the two of you are ready, let us know. We'll make the official announcement that there has been a royal engagement."

"Thank you, father."

"We'll celebrate with you both a little more privately later—Sarah's guests, too," my mother adds. "Tell Sarah that we said congratulations." She squeezes my shoulder before they continue making their rounds around the room.

"What did he say about engagement?" asks Charlotte. "And celebrating something?"

I wrap my arm around Sarah's waist, and she beams at them, her eyes sparkling with delight. "Can I tell them?" she asks me excitedly.

"Of course. They should be the first to know before we make our official announcement to the kingdom."

"We're engaged!" she squeals happily, just loud enough for them to hear.

"Oh, that's wonderful, honey!" her mother says, wrapping Sarah in a hug. "We're so happy for you. Both of you." She pulls me into her embrace next.

"Congratulations," adds her father, giving Sarah a hug before patting me on the back. "Welcome to the family, son."

"Thank you, sir. I'll take good care of her."

"I know that you will."

As I watch Sarah happily showing off her ring to her family and friends, I smile to myself, wondering how I ever got so lucky as to have this gorgeous woman sweep me off of my feet, quite literally. She's the best thing that's ever happened to me, and I can't wait to marry her.

THE END

Author's Note

Thank you so much for reading this quick little holiday novella! I had so much fun writing it, and I'm super happy that I get to share this story with all of you. If you enjoyed this story, please take a moment to leave a review on Amazon. I appreciate your support, and I look forward to hearing your feedback.

Also, be sure to sign up for my newsletter at https://www.emorie-cole.com to receive details about upcoming projects, upcoming events, and get access to exclusive content.

Acknowledgments

It's amazing to me that I've once again reached this point. When I began my writing journey, I never realized just how many ideas and storylines that I would have running through my mind, waiting to be written down and shared with others. I'm grateful that I have the opportunity to continue doing what I love, and that I have the support of my family and friends while I do it.

First, I want to thank my wonderful husband for giving me the support to follow my dreams. Without him, my writing wouldn't be possible. He was the one who encouraged me to start writing my own romance novels, and without his encouragement, I wouldn't be where I am today.

He has also been an amazing sounding board for ideas throughout my entire writing journey so far, and a helping hand with editing as he isn't afraid to give me critique and constructive criticism. As always he has created a beautiful book cover for me, and I absolutely love it. A great deal of his free time is spent helping me so that I'm able to produce the best possible books that I can for all of you, and I don't know where I would be without all of his help.

I also want to thank all of my family and friends who continue to support me by reading my stories, sending encouragement, and keeping me on track by continuing to ask when my next book is coming out! I love you guys!

And last, but not least, I can't forget to thank all of you wonderful readers again. Without you, I wouldn't be able to continue creating amazing stories and sharing them with the world.

About the Author

Emorie Cole is a small town girl who grew up in Upper Michigan. She loves to show her creative side through her writing, creating sweet romance stories that are filled with passion and steam so that her readers can be swept into a world where they feel emotional bonds being formed and can find happily ever afters.

When she's not writing, you can find her curled up with a good book, spending time with her family, playing with her dog, and enjoying the Florida sunshine.

Also by Emorie Cole

Standalones

Passion on Waikiki

Resonating Love

Wilkins Harbor Series

(read in any order)

Love at the Inn

Accidental Love

Midnight Carriage Kiss

Other Standalones

Unexpected Love on Christmas Eve: A Second Chance
Romance